The Story & Song of Black Roderick by Dora Sigerson Shorter

Dora Mary Sigerson was born in Dublin on August 16th, 1866, the daughter of George Sigerson, a surgeon and writer, and Hester (née Varian) also a writer.

Her father was a leader in Dublin's intellectual world and immersed the young Dora in the vibrant literary society of Dublin throughout her childhood, helping her gain a deep and complete love of her country. Like her father, Dora was active in the Irish literary revival, and a passionate campaigner for home rule.

Her poetry collections date from 1893 and are particularly evocative when she writes of her homeland, War and, most of all, the Easter Rising of 1916. Her friends included Katharine Tynan, the noted Irish poet and author as well as fellow writers and poets Rose Kavanagh and Alice Furlong

When she married Clement King Shorter, an English journalist and literary critic, in 1895 they moved to England and she wrote under the name Dora Sigerson Shorter. Although in England her heart's passion remained with Ireland.

The tragic events of Easter 1916, were a terrible blow to her and her health quickly began to fail.

Dora Mary Sigerson Shorter died on January 6th, 1918. The cause of her death was not disclosed.

As well as a foremost poet Dora's talents extended to sculpture, journalism and novels.

Dora's best-known sculpture is the memorial in Glasnevin Cemetery to the executed leaders of the Easter Rebellion.

In her lifetime she was renowned for her personal beauty and her charm. That charm is reflected in her works which are full of eagerness, love, sympathy, and, of course, suffering.

Index of Contents

The Story and Song of Black Roderick

This is the story of Black Earl Roderick, the story and the song of his pride and of his humbling; of the bitterness of his heart, and of the love that came to it at last; of his threatened destruction, and the strange and wonderful way of his salvation.

So shall I begin and tell.

He left his gray castle at the dawn of the morning, and with many a knight to bear him company rode, not eager and swift, like a prince who went to find a treasure, but steady and slow, as we should go to meet sorrow. Not one of the hundred men who followed dared to lilt a lay or fling a laughing jest from his mouth. All rode silent among their gay trappings, for so saith a song:

It was the Black Earl Roderick
Who rode towards the south;
The frown was heavy on his brow,
The sneer upon his mouth.

Behind him rode a hundred men
All gay with plume and spear;
But not a one did lilt a song
His weary way to cheer.

So stern was Black Earl Roderick
Upon his wedding-day,
To none he spake a single word
Who met him on his way.

And of those that passed him as he went there were none who dared to bid him God-speed, and only one whispered at all; she was Mora of the Knowledge, who was picking herbs in a lonely place and saw him ride.

"There goeth the hunter," said she; "'tis a white doe that thou wouldst kill. High hanging to thee, my lord, upon a windy day!"

And of all the flying things he met in his going, one only dared to put pain upon him, and she was a honeybee who stabbed his cheek with her sword.

"Would I could slay thee," she cried, "ere thou rob the hive of its honey!"

And of all the creeping things that passed him on his way, only one tried to stay him; she was the bramble who cast her thorn across his path so his steed wellnigh stumbled.

"Would I could make thee fall, Black Earl, who now art so high, ere thou rob fruit from the branch!"

Only one living thing upon the mountains saw him go without mourning, and he was the red weasel who took the world as he found it.

"Tears will not heal a wound," saith he, "but they will quench a fire. Thy hive is in danger, bee," quoth he. "Bramble, thy flowers are scattered and thy fruit lost."

But the Black Earl did not heed or hear anything outside his own thoughts. They were sharper than the bee's sword and less easy to cast aside than the entrapping bramble.

When he reached the castle wherein his bride did dwell, he blew three blasts upon the horn that hung beside the gate, and in answer to his call a voice cried out to him. But what it said I shall sing thee, lest thou grow weary of my prose:

"Come in, come in, Earl Roderick,
Come in or you be late;
The priest is ready in his stole.
The wedding guests await."

And then the stern Earl Roderick
From his fierce steed came down;
The sneer still curled upon his lip,
His eyes still held the frown.

He strode right haughtily and quick
Into the banquet-hall,
And stood among the wedding guests,
The greatest of them all.

He gave scant greeting to the throng,
He waved the guests aside:
"Now haste! for I, Earl Roderick,
Will wait long for no bride!

"And I must in the saddle be
Before the night is gray;
So quickly with the marriage lines,
And let us ride away."

And now shall I tell thee how, as he spoke thus proud and heartlessly, his little bride came into the hall? So white was she, and so trembled she, that many wondered she did not sink upon the marble floor and die.

Her mother held her snow-white hand, weeping bitterly the while.

"If I had my will," thought she, "this thing should never be. Oh, sharp sorrow," sobbed she, "this for a woman: my trouble thou art, and my thousand treasures."

Her father, seeing the frowning Earl, muttered in his beard:

"Would there were some other way. Stern is he and hard, to wear a young maid's heart." And then aloud he spoke, laying his hands upon the yellow curls of his child: "This is the golden link that binds the clans. God's sweet love be upon her head, for she hath healed a cruel and evil quarrel between the two houses. Lift up your voices, my comrades, and make ye merry; it is a good deed you have helped in to-day."

Now, when the guests turned with their laughter and gentle jesting to the newly married pair, the Black Earl relented not his frown. With scant courtesy and brief good-bye he mounted upon his fretting steed, vowing he could no longer stay. Up before him they lifted the young bride.

"'Tis a rough place to carry the child," wept the sad mother.

But her father smiled upon the Black Earl.

"Where but upon his heart should she rest? Is that not so, my son?"

"If it be not cold," muttered the sullen bridegroom, drawing his rein.

"Wrap thy cloak about her," cried the father, waving farewell.

"Wrap thy love about her," wept the mother, hiding her face.

So rode the Black Earl and his bride, followed by his sullen men-at-arms, gay with their wedding favors.

To his weary little bride he spoke no gentle word, though she fluttered weeping upon his breast like to some wounded thing.

For in his heart the gloomy Earl spake bitterly, and said he:

"Not upon thy hand did I hope to place my golden ring; I have put my own true love aside, to keep the clans together, and wedding thee thus have I been false to the desires of my heart, so do I turn from thee who art my bride."

Thus did he take her to his castle in silence, and, lifting her from his steed, bid her enter the strong gates before him.

So shut they with a clang upon her youth and her merry heart, and she became the neglected mistress of the gray towers she had looked on from afar, and bride of the great Earl she had dreamed of so long.

But to the Black Roderick she was as nothing; he sought her not, neither did he speak of her; she was but the cruel small hand that closed upon his heart and drew it from its love, claiming him in honor her own. And to her claim was he faithful, turning even his thoughts away, lest he should be false to his vow. But no more than this did he give her.

So was she left alone, the young bride who did not understand a man's ways, and, fearing where she loved, hid from his presence lest he should look upon her in hate. Oft had she dreamed of the wonder of being the wife of this proud Earl, in trembling desire and hope, hearing her parents speak of him and of the troth. Oft had she listened to their murmured words, as they spoke of the clans and the peace these two could bring.

"Stern he is, and black for the young child," said her mother, "and I am afraid"; but the child stole away to the hill behind her father's castle, and there looked into the valley of Baile-ata-Cliat to watch the white towers of the Black Earl glistening in the sun, to dream and to tremble.

And as she gazed a honey-bee hummed in her ear, "Go not to the great city."

And as she smiled she raised her hand between her eyes and the far-off towers so she could not see.

"Nay," quoth she, "it is a small place; my hand can cover it."

"Ring a chime," saith she to the heather shaking its bells in the wind, "ring for me a wedding chime, for I am to be the bride of the Earl Roderick."

She kissed the wild bramble lifting its petals in the sun.

"I shall return to thee soon."

And so, springing to her feet, she ran laughing down the hill, and as she ran the spirit of the hills was with her, blowing in her eyes and lifting her soft hair.

"I shall return to thee soon," she said again, and so entered her father's house and prepared herself for her betrothed.

What of her dream was there now? She was indeed the Earl's bride, but, alack! she was divorced from his heart and was naught to his days.

Never did she sit by his knee when he drew his chair by the fire, weary from the chase, nor lean beside him while he slept, to wonder at her happiness. Down the great halls she went, looking through the narrow windows on the outside world, as a brown moth flutters at the pane, weary of an imprisonment that had in its hold the breath of death.

Weary and pale grew she, and more morose and stern the Black Earl, and of their tragedy there seemed no end. But when a year had nigh passed, one rosy morning a servant-lass met Black Roderick as he came from his chamber, her eyes heavy with tears.

And of what she said I shall sing, lest thou grow weary of my prose:

"Alas!" she said, "Earl Roderick,
'Tis well that you should know
That each gray eve, lone wandering,
My mistress dear doth go.

"She comes with sorrow in her eyes
Home in the dawning light;
My lord, she is so weak and young
To travel in the night."

Now stern grew Black Earl Roderick,
But answered not at all;
He took his hunting harness down
That hung upon the wall.

Then quickly went he to the chase,
And slowly came he back,
And there he met his old sweetheart,
Who stood across his track.

So shall I tell how she, sighing and white of face, laid her soft hand upon his bridle-rein so he could not go from her. Her breath came out of her like the hissing of a trodden snake, poisoning the ear of the horseman.

"Bend to me thy proud head, Black Earl," quoth she, "for it shall be low enough soon. This is a tale I bring to thee of sorrow and shame. Bend me thy proud neck, Black Roderick, for the burden I must lay upon it shall bow thee as the snow does the mountain pine. Bend to me thine ear."

To him then she said:

"Where goeth your mistress?"

"What care I?" said the Black Earl, "since she be not thou."

"If she were I," said his lost love, "she would seek no other save thee alone."

"What sayest thou?" said the Black Earl, pale as death.

"Each night she goeth through the woods of Glenasmole to the hill of brown Kippure, and there lingereth until the dawn be chill."

"Who hath her love?" saith the Black Earl.

"A shepherd, or mayhap a swineherd--who knoweth?" quoth the serpent voice. "By no brave prince art thou supplanted."

At this the Black Earl struck his hand upon his breast.

"Lord pity me," quoth he, "that in my time should come the stain upon our honored house! My name, that was so white, shall now blush red. My proud ancestors will curse me from their tomb. Let thou go my rein, that I may seek this wanton and give her ready punishment."

So quick he drew the rein from her hand that she wellnigh stumbled. And like one bereft of mind he rode through the woods and up the hill seeking his false bride. High and low he searched, but no sign of his lost mistress did he discover. Out in the distance he saw the shining city of Baile-ata-Cliat, on the near wood side of which his gray towers stood. He could see the flag on its topmost turret waving in the breeze like a beckoning finger calling him back from his futile search. He turned him about, and on every side of him were the shadowy mountains watching him and appalling him with their mystery. Impatient he turned his eyes upon the ground; a bramble moving in the wind cast itself about his feet. He crushed it under his heel. A bee darting from one of the trodden flowers made a battle-cry, and bared her sting for his neck. He struck it down among the leaves; following its fall, his eyes, drawn by some other eyes, rested on a hollow by a stone. There he saw gazing at him the whiskered face of a red weasel, looking without pity, without fear.

"Evil beast!" said the Black Earl, glad to speak, for the silence of all the listening things who watched him made his heart beat with unwonted quickness, and he knew they were so many silent judges reading the evil of his soul. "Get thee gone," quoth the Black Earl. "Darest thou gaze upon me without fear?"

But the red weasel, resting at the doorway of his hole, did not blink a lid of his sharp eyes.

"Who art thou that evil should droop ashamed before thee?" said a voice, and the Black Earl turned as though a stone had struck him.

Now, when he looked east and west, no one could he see, but when he turned him south, there among the trees he saw an old, bent woman gathering herbs. He turned his horse and, full of rage, drove it towards her.

"Was it not thy voice that hurt my ears as I stood upon the hill?" quoth the Black Earl, his tongue silken in his rage.

"Nay," said the ancient crone; "I heard but the linnet's song upon the tree, and the sound of running water that is murmuring in the grove. Listen, and thou, too, shalt hear."

"Nay," quoth she again, for the Black Earl scowled so at her that she feared to be silent. "If I said this thing, why should it vex the ear of so proud a knight? Yonder black rook did look into my face with an inquisitive eye as I plucked my herbs and harmed no man, so I, angry at the wicked one, cursed him begone. As he flew affrighted at my hand, I turned my eyes into my own heart. The birds and I, do we not both root in the cold earth, seeking to draw from it our desires? Black and ill-looking, we dig all day. 'Who art thou,' quoth I to myself, 'that evil should fly before thee?' Wicked that I am," cried the witch, "and sorrow upon me that my words have vexed thine ears!"

Now the Black Earl did look upon her in anger, and but half believed her tale. His trouble being heavy upon him, he bade her leave her lamenting and answer his question.

"There is one," quoth he, "who doth wander upon the hill-side, far from her home, a lady of high degree; sawest thou any such," saith he, "for I have sought her long?"

Now will I sing thee what was said and what happened, lest thou grow weary of my prose:

"I have not seen your lady here,"
The withered dame replied;
"But I have met a little lass
Who wrung her hands and cried.

"She was not clad in silken robe,
Nor rode a palfrey white,
She had no maidens in her train,
Behind her rode no knight.

"But she crept weary up yon hill
And crouched upon the sward;

I dare not think that she could be
Spouse to so great a lord."

Now darkly frowned Earl Roderick,
He turned his face away;
And shame and anger in his heart
Disturbed him with their sway.

For he had never cared to know
What his young bride would wear;
He gave her neither horse nor hound,
Nor jewels for her hair.

Now shall I tell how the Black Earl clapped his hand upon his dagger, and said in a great rage: "Where went this little lass, and whom hath she by her side? for whoever he be, I shall show to him no pity. Neither shall her tears save her. Nor shall thy age serve thee, witch, if thou hast spoken not the truth. Whither went they, so I may follow, as the hound goes on the trail of the deer?"

"Oh, sharp sorrow thy anger is!" cried the old crone; "what can I say, save what my eye hath seen and my ear hath heard? The little lass passed me as I gathered my herbs under the dew. She hath by her side no lord nor lover. She went sad and alone. Here climbed she the height of the hill, and there sat she making her lament."

"And what lament made she?" said the Black Earl, putting his dagger into its sheath.

"Once called she on her father, as one who drowns in deep waters would call upon a passing ship. Twice called she upon her mother, as one would call upon a house of rest or of hospitality. Thrice called she upon Earl Roderick, as one would call at the gates of paradise, there to find rescue and love."

"And said she naught else?" said the Black Earl, his head upon his breast.

"Yea," quoth the crone, "when she called upon her father, she smiled through her tears. 'Didst thou know I perish,' quoth she, 'thy arms would reach to save me!'

"And when she called twice upon her mother, her mouth smiled even the same, 'for didst thou learn my hunger, thy heart would warm me to life again'; but when she called three times upon Earl Roderick, she paused as though for an answer, and smiled no more. 'Thee,' quoth she, 'I perish for, I hunger for. Thou lovest me not at all.'

"So did she sit and make her moan upon the hill, and here watched she the lights in the far windows of her lost home quench themselves one by one. 'Now,' quoth she, 'my mother sleepeth, and now my father. And now by all am I forgotten.' Then did she steal, in the dim light, down from the hill, and I saw her no more."

"What didst thou tell to her, old witch?" quoth the Black Earl, "as she passed weeping? Didst thou speak to her no word?"

"I stopped her as she passed me, proud Earl," quoth the crone, "for she was gentle, and held her head not too high to look upon one old and near unto death.

"'Weep not,' said I, 'but spread to me thy fingers, so I may read what fate thou holdest in thy palm.' And like a child she smiled between her tears.

"'Look only on luck,' quoth she, 'oh, ancient one, lest my heart break even now.' I spread her pink fingertips out as one would unruffle a rose, and read therein her fate."

"And what read you there?" said the Black Earl, impatient with her delay.

"I read," quoth the crone, "and if I say, thou must keep thy anger from me, for what I read I had not written:

"I traced upon her slender palm
That luck was changing soon;
I swore that peace would come to her
Before another moon.

"I said that he who loved her well
Would robe her all in silk,
And bear her in a coach of gold,
With palfreys white as milk.

"I told, before three suns had set
He'd kneel down by her side;
That he she loved would love her well,
And she would be his bride.

"'This before three suns have set,' so read I," quoth the crone.

Now, when the Black Earl heard so much, he would hear no more. Pallid grew his angry cheek, and his eyes were full of fire; he flung himself upon his horse, and, sparing not the beast, galloped home.

"In the highest tower shall I lock the jade," quoth he, "lest she bring me shame; for what her palm had writ upon it one must believe, and who dare love her, save I who will not? And should I die, wherefore should she not be another's? And should I not die--but this no man dare, for I shall tear his tongue from his mouth, his ear from his cheek, his heart from his body, ere he speak or listen to a word to my dishonor."

Now, when he reached his castle, no man ventured to speak to him, or look upon him with too inquisitive an eye, for his anger was such that one trembled to approach him.

And at the gate of his castle sat his old love upon her palfrey, with a stern face and grim; behind her, resting upon their way, came her followers, knight and lady, gay with banner and spear, whispering in their telling of the story.

"A curse upon the wandering feet that have brought disgrace upon thy house," quoth his old love, her hand so tight upon the rein that the two pages could hardly keep the horse from rearing.

But the proud Earl to her made no answer, neither to bid her welcome, nor to bid her go, nor to speak of his fears. Into his breast he locked his grief so that none might know the strain wellnigh broke the stony casket of his heart.

When he leaped from his horse there came to him his little brother.

"My grief!" said the boy, "what has happened in the night, for I heard the banshee sobbing so bitterly through the dark?"

No answer made the Black Earl to the boy, neither did he lift him in his arms nor chide him for his weeping, but passed silent into his own chamber, and crouched within his chair. When after a time he raised his eyes, he seemed to see his young bride gazing upon him from the open door. And in his anger he sprang to seize her, but only the empty air came to his hands.

He mounted the marble stairs to her chamber to seek her there, but only found a sewing-maid, pale and deadly faint.

"Oh, sharp sorrow," quoth she, "from what I have seen this night, Mary protect me! A white ghost have I seen--evil it may bring to me--a white ghost with dim eyes of the dead!"

"Whither went she?" said the Black Earl, angry in his need.

"Into thy chamber, great Earl!" cried the maid; "I saw her at thy bed-head weeping piteously."

"It was thy lady," quoth the Earl; "lead me her way, and stop thy lamentation."

"My grief!" the girl said, "her way I know not; when I, deeming her my mistress, reached her side, she was no more. It is an evil day that cometh upon us."

Now, when the proud Roderick saw the girl so full of fear, he chid her cruelly and bade her go. Yet when she had left him he felt a strange and unwonted coldness settle upon his heart.

The anger against his young bride was quenched, and a dewlike fear grew upon him. But of what befell him I shall now sing to thee, lest thou grow weary of my prose:

All silent Black Earl Roderick
Went to his room away,
Full angry, with his throbbing heart
And fitful fancy's play.

He sat him by the bright hearth-side,
And turned towards the door;
And there upon the threshold stood
His lady, weeping sore.

He chased her down the winding stair,
And out into the night,
But only found a withered crone,
With long hair, loose and white.

"Come hither now, you sly-faced witch;
Come hither now to me.
Say if a lady all so pale
Your evil eyes did see?"

"Oh, true, I saw a little lass,
She went all white as snow;
She crossed my hands with silver crown
Just two short hours ago."

"What did you tell the foolish wench,
Who must my lady be?
The false tale you did tell to her
You now must tell to me."

"I hate you, Black Earl Roderick,
You're cruel, hard, and cold;
Yet you shall grieve like a young child
Before the moon is cold.

"This did I tell her, like a queen
She'd ride into the town;
And every man who met her there
Would on his knees go down.

"I said that he who followed none
Would walk behind her now,
And in his trembling hand the helm
From his uncovered brow.

"Then he should walk, while she would ride,
Through all the town away;
And greater than Earl Roderick
She would become that day."

And now shall I tell how laughed the Black Earl aloud and scornful at the witch's tale.

"No lady in the land," quoth he, "could so enslave me, and no woman yet was born who hath my honor and glory."

So spoke Earl Roderick, and by these words shalt thou hold him, heart-whole and vain withal, for the hour of his sorrow had not yet struck.

Now turned he to the dame, and, chiding her, bade her begone.

"Thy tale," saith he, "is full of weariness. It hath neither wisdom nor truth."

Turning from her in anger, home went he, and flung himself before the dying fire in his chamber, a frown between his brows. And again a cold fear turned closely about his heart. Raising his eyes, he saw no more terrible a thing than his young bride, with a face of grievous pain, looking upon him from the door. Then he spoke her gently.

"Come," quoth he, "sad-faced one, why dost thou torment me? One question only shall I ask thee, and this must thou answer. Whom hast thou met upon the hill? For the witch woman hath told me a wearisome tale, which I shall not lend my ear to."

Now, when he spoke, his young bride neither answered nor came, but gazed from the threshold upon him in silence. So he got up in anger and went her way. Through the chamber strode he, and she was yet before him, and without sound went she down the hall and stair. So out through the open door, and the men-at-arms let her pass, though the Black Earl bid them stay her feet, and gazed bewildered, seeing only their stern master running alone, with fierce eyes, such as a hound doth cast upon a young hare. Quick as the Black Earl ran, the little bride was before.

Through sleepy woods and honey-perfumed plains, all through the night did he chase her, but never once did he reach her, nor ever once did she pause to rest.

When the morning sun was high, she led him up to the lights of Brown Kippure, and there vanished from his sight.

Now, when the Black Earl perceived this wondrous thing, he felt his heart sink with utter weariness, and without more seeking fell upon the moss. Had his eyes been not so hot with anger, slow tears of sorrow would have forced their way upon his cheeks, for now that he had her not his desire was strong upon him to behold his bride.

As he lay upon the heather, he heard the shrill voice of his little brother clamoring by his side.

"Be still," quoth he, "for thou hast frightened away a fair dream that I fain would follow."

"But I would tell thee," said the little brother, "of a strange thing, and one to set thee full of laughter."

"Nay," quoth the Black Earl, "of that I have no desire, lest thou place upon my head a cap and bells, and call me fool Roderick."

"And wherefore," said the little brother, "shouldst thou laugh at fool Roderick?"

"Because," quoth the Black Earl, "he hath found a strange jewel when he hath lost it."

"Thy words I do not understand," saith the little brother. "What was the strange jewel that he hath and yet hath not?"

"Love," quoth the Black Earl.

"That neither do I understand," saith the little brother, "but now thou must listen to my story."

And of what he saith shall I sing, for his voice was sweeter than prose:

"Oh, brother, brother, come up to the lake waters gray,
Come up to the shore where I play;
For, oh! I saw on the bank asleep
A fair white nymph, and the slow waves creep,
To bear her away, away.

"Oh, brother, brother, I watched her through the day,
Saw her hair grow jewelled with spray.
Once her cheek was brushed by a robin's wing,
And a finch flew down on her hand to sing,
And was not afraid to stay.

"Oh, brother, brother, will she soon awaken be?
I would that she laugh with me.
She sleeps, and the world so full of sound;
She's deaf, like the deaths that are under the ground,
That I laugh and laugh to see."

Now shall I tell how the Black Earl heeded not the story of the little brother, nor the tragedy that lay therein, for his ear was busy with another sound.

"Hush," said the Black Earl, "for hearest thou not a voice in trouble?"

"Nay," cried the little brother; "I hear naught save the laughing stream that comes from the lake where my water-nymph lieth."

"Hush!" said the Black Earl again, "for hearest thou not the voice of my mistress making a lamentation?"

"Nay," saith the little brother; "I hear naught save the moving of the reeds in the pushing waters, and thou wilt not listen to my story."

Now went the little brother away in his anger, and found himself a play among the heather.

But the Black Earl bent above the stream and gazed long into its shallow turbulence with wonder and fear, for the words the stream said to him in its whisperings were as though spoken in the voice of his young bride.

He laid his hand in the flowing waters.

"Why art thou troubled, little stream?" quoth he.

But the little stream stayed not its whispering.

"Sainted Mother, oh, pray for me!" it murmured, in piteous prayer, "and leave sweet mercy upon my soul."

Now, when the Black Earl heard the voice of his lady coming from the waters in such sorrow, he rose with a cry, and, his heart being full of fear, he knew at last the greatness of his love.

"Where art thou, then?" he cried, in his woe. "Whither shall I seek thee?"

But the little stream passing his feet murmured its prayer in going; no other sound did he hear save the far-away laughter of his little brother.

"Oh, Mary, Mother, pray my soul to rest! Take mercy, Lord, on a soul afraid."

"Where are the lips from which thou hast stolen that cry?" said the Black Earl; and, like an old man bent with trouble, he sought the banks, seeking for the white form of his bride. "Now," quoth he, "well do I know this stream hath carried her last cry to my feet, and her drowning lips have been forced to sinful death to-night by my long cruelty."

He went up the hill as a man goeth to despair, slow and afraid; and when he reached the little wood in whose bosom the lake was enshrined, he paused and looked around.

Of this shall I sing, for so sad and piteous it is that my harp would fain soothe me from tears:

He looked into the deep wood green,
But nothing there did see;
He looked into the still water
Beneath, all white, lay she.

He drew her from her cold, cold bed,
And kissed her cheek and chin;
Loosed from his neck his silken cloak,
To wrap her body in.

He took her up in his two arms--
His grief was deep and wild;
He knelt beside her on the sod,
And sorrowed like a child.

He blew three blasts upon his horn;
His men did make reply,
And came all quickly to his call,
Through brake and brier so high.

And every man who saw her there
Went down upon his knee;
Behind her came Earl Roderick,
All pitiful to see.

And in his trembling hand the helm
From his uncovered brow;
And "Oh," he said, "to love her well,
And know it only now!"

So he did walk while she did ride
Through all the town away,
For greater than Earl Roderick
She did become that day.

Now have I said how the heart of the Black Earl woke to love, and then was humbled, as the ancient crone had foretold; but of his sorrowful years, his desperate danger of eternal loss and his after-salvation, must I likewise tell, if the story would be pitiful in the ending.

Therefore shall I lay my harp aside, and so go back in my telling.

And I bid thee remember how the little pale bride was wont to sit upon the mountain and watch the far lights in her father's home quench themselves one by one.

So now of how she died shall I tell thee, and of what came to her in her passing, lest thou thinkest so innocent a child had laid violent hands upon her life, who only had met death through the breaking of her heart.

Here sat she on the mountain, and the wild things spoke of her in her silence. The red weasel, the bee, and the bramble, and many others, moved to watch her. Well have they known her in her young joyfulness; here had she made the place she loved best--the high brow of the hill where she sat as a child and watched--on the one side the far-off city and the white towers that held the wonder-knight of her dreams. Here had she sat and seen the gleam of his spear as he went with his hunters through the valley; and here, too, had her mother come to tell her of her betrothal, so she had nigh fainted in her happiness, in looking upon the white tower that was to be her home.

Here had she learned the sweet language of the birds and flowers, and they, too, had partaken of her joys; but of her sorrows they would not understand, for our joys and our laughter, are they not as the singing of the bird and the dancing of the fly, who weep only when they meet death? In our griefs do we not stand alone, who have in our hearts the fierce desires of love and all the tragedies of despair?

Now, as the young bride turned her slow feet up the mountain, down where her glad feet had turned as a maid, she sat her there by the lake.

The little creatures she was wont to love and understand gathered about her and wondered at her state.

"She hath returned," said the red weasel; "see where she sitteth, her head upon her hand. I slew a young bird at her feet, and she spake no word, nor did she care."

"It is not she," said a linnet, swaying on a safe spray, "for had it been she her anger would have slain thee."

"It is she," said the red weasel, laughing in his throat; "but her eyes are hidden by her fingers, and she cannot see."

"It is not she," said a brown wren. "Her cheek was full and rosy and her song loud. This one sitteth all mute and pale."

"It is she," said the red weasel, "who sitteth upon the mountain, her face hidden between her hands. She sitteth in silence, and who can tell her thoughts? She hath been to the great city."

"It is a small place," hummed a honey-bee. "Once, long ago, she raised her white palm between her eyes and its smoke. 'See,' she laughed, 'my little hand can cover it.'"

"It is so great," said the red weasel, "that those who leave the mountains for love of it return to us no more."

"Yet she hath returned," said a lone lark hanging in the sky, "and I myself have sung beside her ear."

"She came, yet she came not," said the red weasel. "What did she answer when thou saidst that I had slain thy mate?"

"She sighed, 'Thou singest a gay song, O bird!'" hummed a golden beetle. "My grief! that she cannot understand."

"She is lost to us indeed!" said a honeysuckle swaying in the wind, "for she trod me beneath her feet when I held my sweet blossoms for her lips."

"And she tore me aside," cried the wild bramble, "when I did but reach towards her for embrace."

"She will know thee no more," said the red weasel; "she hath been to the great city."

"She laid her lips upon me ere she went," spake the wild bramble, "and said she would return to us soon."

"She bid me ring a merry chime," whispered the heather, "and I move my many bells now for her welcome, but she will not hear."

"She will speak with thee no more," said the red weasel; "she hath walked in the city, like one goeth upon the fairy sleeping grass, and her soul hath forgotten us."

"She is still and cold," said a shining fly glancing through the air. "I have danced a measure under her eyes, and she did not see."

"She is dead," said the honey-bee, "for when she would not look upon me as before, I drew my sword and stung her sharply, but she did not stir. She sat and gazed into the distance where the smoke like a great gray web lieth heavy. She is surely dead."

"She is not dead," said the red weasel; "she hath been to the great city."

"Maybe there she hath found Death," said the shining fly, "for his web reacheth far, and he loveth the dark places and hidden ways. He hideth, too, in the cool arbors of the wood, stretching a gray chain for our undoing. Maybe she found Death. He spreadeth ropes of pearls across our path, and looketh upon us from the shade; when the dance is gayest he creepeth to spring. Maybe she hath reached for the pearls or hath danced into his net."

And so the fly sang of the watcher in the wood, and his song I shall sing thee, lest thou grow weary of my prose:

Deep in the wood's recesses cool
I see the fairy dancers glide,
In cloth of gold, in gown of green,
My lord and lady side by side.

But who has hung from leaf to leaf,
From flower to flower, a silken twine,
A cloud of gray that holds the dew
In globes of clear enchanted wine,

Or stretches far from branch to branch,
From thorn to thorn, in diamond rain?
Who caught the cup of crystal wine
And hung so fair the shining chain?

'Tis death the spider, in his net,
Who lures the dancers as they glide,
In cloth of gold, in gown of green,
My lord and lady side by side.

But a dragon-fly rattling his armor said, without heed of the singer, "She is dead," for when she came among the heather the joyous spirit of the mountain met her and blew upon her hair and eyes. He kissed her worn cheek that he had known so fair, and the soft rain of his sorrow fell to see the pity of her brow. She passed all stiff and cold; she did not hear nor understand.

"Wind," quoth she, "blow not so fierce."

"She is not dead," saith the red weasel; "she hath been to the great city."

Now, when the young bride raised her white face from her hands and looked about her, she could neither hear the speaking of the birds nor see the beauty of the wild flowers, yet in her heart she had a memory of both. Turning to the little flying things that came about her with soft, beating wings, she said:

"Once ye spake to me, and could give comfort with your counsel and love. Now ye are lost in the voices of the city that ring forever in my ears."

Gazing upon the flowers, she said:

"Ye, too, your beauty hath faded. The gaudy flowers of the city have flashed their color in my eyes, so ye I cannot see or understand."

Then she rose to her feet, though she scarce could stand, and, stretching her arms towards the great purple hills that surrounded her father's far home, she said towards it:

"Why didst thou call me back since thou hast let me go from the sight of the heights that would have been always a prayer to uplift my soul? Ahone! that thy voice was loud enough to follow and give me unrest, that whispered always of my father's house and the valley of my home. So must I come each eve upon this hill to look upon it from my loneliness.

"Unloved am I, and unwished for, by him whom I have wedded. So my heart dieth within my breast, and my soul trembleth on the brink of my grave.

"Here upon the mountains, unprayed for and uncoffined, shall my body lie, for thy voice hath called me forth.

"Here my black sins shall see and pursue me even to destruction; but in the city I could have escaped with the crowding souls that confuse Death to count."

Then, as a remembrance of her sins came heavy upon her, she gave a loud cry and covered her face with her hands.

So she stood without help upon the mountains, and because she was blind with the city dust and deafened with its cries, she stood alone. The pitying wild flowers blew their fragrance to her eyes, but they would not open; the gentle birds spoke comforting whispers to her ears, but she could not hear; the great hills held their arms about her and breathed their peace upon her brow. But this she did not know, and so stood alone to face Death.

First turned she her face to where her father's castle stood on a far hill, and again turned she to see the white towers where she had lived and loved so vainly. And when her eyes met the glisten of the walls, her heart broke with a little sigh, and she fell upon the ground. And she laid her weary body down beside the waters of the mountain lake. Her head with its loosened hair lay in the waters, so her lips, covered by the murmuring ripples, breathed a prayer as she died for her passing soul. And the little stream that ran from the lake down the hill-side carried the prayer upon its breast as thou hast been told.

Now, when the ghost of the little bride stood upright beside her fallen body, she was sore afraid, and trembled much to leave the habitation she had known in life.

She laid her spirit-hands upon the cold dead, and clung to it as though she would not be driven forth. Many and terrifying were the sights that met her when she opened her eyes, after passing through the change of death. Many and terrifying were the sounds that came to her ears, and she feared she would be whirled away with the great clouds that passed her and went like smoke into the skies. Cold she was and drenched with the rain that fell everywhere around her; gray and misshapen were the moving masses under her gaze; and only where her hands lay holding to her dead body did she see aught of the world she had left behind. There the sweet green grass lifted itself and a brier rose cast its blossom apart. There a bee sang, calling to her a little comfort among all the strange sounds that filled her ears.

As she listened, she found the noises that troubled her were the cries of many voices, and as she began to see more clearly in the great change that had come to her, she knew the shadowy clouds rushing upward were the spirits of the dead on their dangerous swift way to heaven. And as she raised her face to follow their flight the rain fell salt into her mouth, so she knew it was the repentant tears of the passing ghosts.

So crouched she in that misty world, seeing not the green earth and the purple hills, but only the whirling shapes about her on every side, flying from earth to heaven, pursued by their black sins.

And one in the valley of Baile-ata-Cliat, looking towards the mountains, said:

"See how the clouds fly black and fearful!" But it was the hosts of spirits flying upward. "See," quoth he, "how the lightning flashes!" But it was the opening of God's High Paradise to receive some spirit wellnigh spent. "Hark," said he, "how the wind moans and the rain beats upon the window!" But it was the cry of the passing ghosts and their falling tears as their black sins fought and kept them from heaven.

But one who was a singer took his harp and sang, for he understood. Here is his song:

They say it is the wind in midnight skies,
Loud shrieking past the window, that doth make
Each casement shudder with its storm of cries,
And the barred door with pushing shoulder shake.

Ah no, ah no, it is the souls pass by,
Their lot to run from earth to God's high place,
Pursued by each black sin that death let fly
From their sad flesh, to break them in the chase.

They say it is the rain from leaf to leaf
Doth slip and roll into the thirsting ground,
That where the corn is trampled sheaf by sheaf
The heavy sorrow of the storm is found.

Ah no, ah no, it is repentant tears,
By those let fall who make their direful flight,
And drop by drop the anguish of their fears

Comes down around us all the awful night.

They say that in the lightning-flash, and roar
Of clashing clouds, the tempest is about;
And draw their chairs the glowing hearth before,
And casement close to shut the danger out.

Ah no! the doors of Paradise they swing
A moment open for a soul nigh spent,

Then come together till the thunder's ring
Leaves us half blinded by God's element.

Now, the spirit of the young bride was not yet called upon to join their terrible flight, for until her body was laid beneath the clay the soul had power to stay beside it. So stayed the spirit of the young bride by her dead body till her ghostly eyes grew accustomed to the change which had come to her. And when she found she could see the brown earth again and the things thereon, she rose to her feet, and ran down the mountains to the castle of Black Roderick, and there called thrice beside the gate, and for her it was opened by the little brother, who gazed affrighted and ran from her.

"What hath come to thee?" quoth she, and came upon him in his fear.

And he looked not to her, but spake to a knight-at-arms, saying thus:

"Three times cried the voice of my brother's wife at the gates, and when I opened for her there was none outside."

So the little bride, hearing, cried out in her despair, for she had forgotten that she was no longer as these others.

And when the two heard the cry, they were affrighted, and made the cross upon their foreheads.

"It is the banshee," quoth the knight, "who weeps for some death."

Seeing they feared her, the little bride passed sadly into the castle, and timidly sought the chamber where the Black Earl was gone to crouch by the glowing fire.

Now, when Black Roderick looked up and saw her, he sprang towards her so she was afraid, and flitted before him like a shadow. And when he followed up the stair and into his own chamber, she faded like a shadow in the sunshine that came through the window, and the wind, coming down from the mountains and passing through the casement, drew her out upon its breast, and bore her back to the hills where her body lay awaiting its burial.

And seeing it there, a misery fell upon her, so she raised her head and wept.

"Ahone!" quoth she, "poor body that hath no one to weep over thy loneliness, that must lie uncoffined and unprayed for, who wast so tenderly cared for in thy life! Where art thou, my father, where art thou, my mother, that this should be? And where is he to whom this poor body was given to cherish and to love?"

And again she went to the castle of Black Roderick, and stood beside his door, the tears undried upon her cheek. And again sprang he towards her, so she was afraid, and flew before him down the winding stair and out into the night, so he could no longer see her.

And again the spirit of the young bride went back to the dead upon the hill-side, and, seeing it unburied and uncoffined, fell into tears.

"Never," saith she, "shall I now reach heaven, if my body lieth without a grave!"

And so sad was her soul at the thought that she went in her despair to the castle of the Black Earl, and stood again upon his threshold full of tears.

And when he looked up and saw her he was no longer fierce, but spake to her gently.

"Come hither," quoth he, "my sad-faced bride. I would but ask thee one question. Come beside my chair."

But she answered him not at all, but withdrew from his presence, as though bidding him follow.

Out into the night he followed, and pursued her without rest, till she almost reached the high hill where her body lay uncoffined.

And when they came in the morning to the little grove upon the side of the mountain, she felt a hand touch the poor, unmourned-for dead, and, with a great fear upon her, vanished from his eyes; so he fell upon the moss in his disappointment and weariness.

But the spirit of the little bride flew to the side of her uncoffined body to protect it from desecration ere her lord had looked upon it. And there she saw the little brother playing by the dead.

And as she came he turned and ran down the mountain, for he had heard the voice of Black Roderick calling; so the spirit of the little bride knew her task was done. And of how the Black Earl found her, and of what he said and did, have I told thee; but of how the spirit of the young bride enwrapped herself about the dead I have not spoken, nor of how she thrilled beneath the embraces of her lord, whose love she had at the last.

When he stood beside her deep grave, that was dug in the little church-yard nigh to the castle, her spirit rose again from her body, and knew her hour of trial had come.

And when the grave was closed and the mourners gone, the spirit stayed by the grave, afraid.

When evening came, the spirits of the dead rose in a white mist, each above his grave, and all prepared for their swift and dangerous flight towards the dark heavens.

"Now," saith she, "my body can no longer protect me with its earthly presence. I am separated from the world, and am no more of it. I must arise and meet death alone."

The first thing she knew of the great presence was a loud whirring of wings; she raised her head, and saw around her a crowd of evil birds. So afraid was she that she gave a loud and sudden cry, and at the sound the ill birds rose and hovered in the air between her and heaven.

"My sins have discovered me," she cried, "and now I fear death!"

And because she knew that before dawn she would have to account for her evil deeds, she lifted up her voice in loud keening. So sad was her cry that the pitying wind bore it down upon his wings into the little village at the foot of the mountain, that the people might hear and pray for a soul in its passing.

But the people in the village were busy even so late with the harvest, and did not hear; only in one house where a mother sat with her sick child did the cry come, and she closed the shutter and fell to prayer.

"'Tis the banshee who crieth," she whispered, "and my Conneen so ill! 'Tis the banshee, and Sheila with the cheek of snow. God bid the fairy pass, and set the angels at my door! Whisht!" she cried to the playing young ones, "come beside my chair and pray."

And of her fear shall I sing, lest thou grow weary of my prose:

Oh, whisht! I hear the banshee keen,
All woful is her cry.
She comes along the gray boreen--
Pray God she pass us by.

My wee Conneen is pale and weak,
I hold him to my side;
The rose is white on Sheila's cheek
Since her young lover died.

The little children from their play
Creep to me full of fear;
"Oh, whisht! the banshee comes," they say:
"Whom does she weep for here?"

But Sheila leaves my chair to go,
And flings the shutter wide;
"Be it for me," she whispers low,
"The banshee keened and cried."

God be between our house and harm,
For trouble comes full fleet.
I hold the babe close in my arm;
The fairy in the street.

But the wind that blew from the hill-side carried the keening of the little bride past the village, and blew it about the windows of the castle wherein Black Roderick dwelt. And as the cry keened and called, so did the sleepers turn in their beds and moan uneasily in their dreaming.

When the cry passed the windows of the east, it went to the windows of the west, and there it tapped softly with fingers of the wind and called three times:

"Roderick! Roderick! Roderick!"

And at the first call Black Roderick turned in his bed and groaned. And at the second call he rose from his couch and said, in his anger:

"Who calleth, and will not let me rest?"

But at the third call he rose and went to the window in wonder, and seeing nothing he crept cold and trembling to his bed, muttering the half-forgotten prayers of his childhood; so long he lay in fear and amazement that he did not sleep till the lark hung singing in the heavens, and then he knew the night was gone and with it the ghosts that hide in the darkness. So he turned his face to the wall and slept. But the spirit of the little bride was speeding on her swift and terrible race to Paradise, and round her whirled three great black birds seeking for her destruction. And as she flew, one caught her by the long hair that swept behind her in the wind and drew her backward.

"Now," quoth she with a cry, "I can fly upward no longer; some evil thing draws me back from heaven."

And as she spoke a voice came out of the dark skies, and said:

"Who holdeth back the passing soul?"

And the voice of the dark bird replied:

"Her anger, for she hath not submitted to her trials, but held herself rebellious; therefore do I draw her down."

And the voice from high paradise called out, saying:

"Is there none to come to her succor, lest she be brought to her destruction?"

And a bee humming on the hillside, hearing the voice, flew upward and stung the evil bird so it fell away into the darkness and was seen no more.

And the voice from the heavens cried again, saying:

"Who hath let the little soul go free?"

And the bee answered:

"Her gentleness, for she loveth all things, great and small, and hath fed the honey-bee when the earth refused him its sweets."

Now, as the spirit of the little bride flew upward, freed from the grasp of the evil bird, there came upon her again the cruel claws of one of those two others that circled round her, holding her back upon her way.

"Now," quoth she, "I shall never see the kingdom of heaven, and cannot reach the doors of paradise," and bitter exceedingly was her crying.

But again a voice came from the dark night, saying:

"Who holdeth back the coming soul from her place in heaven?"

And the black, evil bird answered:

"Her despair, for she hath not held her head high above her sorrows, nor hath borne in patience her griefs, but hath mourned the afflictions that were put upon her till her heart hath broken under her grief. Therefore do I draw her down."

And the voice from high paradise called out, saying:

"Is there none, then, to save her from eternal destruction?"

And a wild bramble upon the mountain, hearing the voice, lifted itself upward, and, throwing a long spray about the evil bird, tore it so with its thorns that it loosed its claws from the wrist of the young bride and flew into the gloom.

And the voice from the heavens cried again, saying:

"Who hath let the soul go free?"

And the bramble answered, wafting the perfume of her flowers upward:

"Her sweetness, for her mind is beautiful as the song of the linnet, and she turneth her foot aside to spare the lowly blossoms."

Now, when once more the spirit of the little bride flew upward, the last and greatest of the evil birds fell upon her, and so strong was he and so evil that she had no strength to go farther.

"Now," quoth she, "I am lost forever, and shall see not the fair place in paradise that was prepared for me." And she gave a loud and despairing cry. But a voice came again from the night, and saith:

"What evil thing keepeth the flying soul upon its way?"

And the dark bird answered:

"Her jealousy, for bitter was her heart against one whom Black Roderick had loved ere she became his bride; and for this do I drag her down to her destruction."

And the voice from the high heavens spoke, saying:

"Is there none, then, to save her?"

And there looked up from the hillside the bright eyes of the red weasel, but he crouched in the grasses without reply. And the grasp of the evil bird became stronger on the quivering soul that could no longer fly upon its way to heaven. And from the great wings of the bird black feathers, wrenched out in the struggle, flew down upon the earth, spreading evil where they fell.

And the voice from heaven cried out again in sorrow exceedingly:

"Is there none, then, to save this soul from destruction?"

And the bee and the bramble, seeing the red weasel was loath to stir from the grasses where he sat watching the desperate battle, fell upon him in their fury and forced him to rise.

"Never," quoth they, "shalt thou have rest, nor thy children's children peace, while there's a bee in the air or a flower upon the thorn, if thou goest not to the succor of her we love so well."

Then the red weasel sprang into the air and seized the evil bird by the throat; so he let go his hold on the spirit of the young bride and flew away into the darkness.

And the voice from heaven cried out, saying:

"Who hath let the frail ghost free to enter the gates of paradise?"

And the red weasel answered:

"Her strength, for she hath conquered her own evil thoughts, and put them away forever."

So the spirit of the young bride reached the gates of paradise spent and wounded, and there upon the threshold stood an angel holding his hand to draw her in.

When his holy touch fell upon her, she rose whole and beautiful, and her breast was full of joy for the moment.

Now, the spirit of the young bride had been but a brief day in the golden place of paradise, when she heard a far voice call upon her name in anguish; three times did it call upon her, and at each cry a sharp sorrow struck her heart, as though a knife had entered therein.

Now went she to the golden bar of heaven, and, leaning forth, looked down upon the earth, and she turned her north, and naught did she see save the cold face of the night with its millions of worlds whirling in the dark. And she looked south, and naught could she see but the gray of clouds heavy with storm; and she turned her east, and naught did she see save the shimmering blue of a summer sky. But when she turned her westward, she saw the green earth, and of all upon it she sought none save Black Roderick, who had used her so ill. And there upon his bed he lay in danger of death, and as he turned in his anguish he called ever upon her name, so her heart knew no longer the peace of paradise, and she became as one of the lost.

Therefore did she rise up and approach the throne where the saints and angels knelt in continual devotion. But she could not see the golden seat, nor HIM who sat thereon. For around and above, and circling ever with rainbow wings, went the seraphim and cherubim in eternal worship, so it was as though a great wheel of light turned continually.

Now, when the spirit of the little bride saw this wonder, she was full of fear and dared not approach, but turned away weeping; and there, as she wept, she saw before her the seat of Mary, the Queen of Heaven, and ran towards it with unfaltering feet.

"For," quoth she, "she, too, had but one love, and, being woman, will understand."

So she knelt at the feet of Mary, and cried to her: "Pray for me, Mother of Christ." And the Virgin turned to her in wonder at her tears.

"Art thou not happy," said she, "in heaven?"

And the spirit of the little bride said: "Nay, for the cries of my beloved come upward from the earth and call to me in his anguish, so I fear he is in danger of death."

"And why doth thou fear death for him," said the Virgin Mary, "since it may bring to him the happiness of heaven?"

"Alas!" said the little bride, "were it thus, his cries would not hurt my heart so that I cannot hear the song of the angels. I fear he is lost forever."

"And what canst thou do, little soul," said the Blessed Mary, "to save him if he cannot save himself?"

"I can be with him in his destruction."

Now, as the little soul said this terrible thing she fell forward upon her face, so afraid was she and so despairing.

"I can stand between him and the flames," said she, "and hold my hand beneath the burning waters that would fall upon his body."

And then she lay silent.

Then the Virgin looked upon her with eyes that were all pitiful and had much understanding.

"Thou wilt suffer," saith she, as though remembering something, "to walk by his side and see his anguish, but thou wouldst suffer more wert thou forbidden this."

So Mary rose from her high place and went towards the high throne of heaven, and as she passed the whirling wings of the seraphim and cherubim ceased to circle, but flew towards her from the throne. And to the little bride, who crouched afraid on the fragrant floor, it seemed as though a great wonder of bees had settled on some hidden sweet; countless wings glistened and flashed in the strange light that glowed from the opening flowers that formed the floor about the throne.

In and out, striking together in their eagerness to get nearer their desire, went the countless wings of the angel hosts.

And from the throne all the time there came forth a low singing like the humming of bees. As the little bride listened there came to her ears the voice of the Virgin praying for her before the throne of God, and in the pauses of the prayer the countless voices of the fluttering seraphim and cherubim took up the refrain, "Hear us, O Christ."

Now suddenly all sound ceased, and the fluttering wings moved aside, and from their midst strode out a mighty angel of the Lord; and when he came upon the frightened soul of the little bride he took her by the hand, and, leading her to the gates of heaven, opened them that she might go forth.

But ere she could pass out he said, with great sadness:

"Thy little hands and feet are soft with the fragrant places of heaven; much wilt thou suffer if thou goest forth."

And again he said:

"How canst thou leave the beauty and love of paradise, wherein thou mayst enter no more save thou art strong enough to conquer great dangers?"

But the little soul listened not to him, but passed through the gates in eager hurry. And as she went the angel followed her with his gaze; and so great was his pity--for he thought she might not re-enter the kingdom of heaven--that tears fell from his eyes upon her hand. Now, when the little bride went forth from the gates of heaven a chill wind blew upon her, so she wellnigh fell upon the earth in anguish; but she took the two tears that had fallen from the angel's eyes and hid them in her heart, and she became warm, and the sharp earth did not hurt her feet, nor did the wind of the cold world harm her.

Now, when the spirit of the little bride came to the gates of the castle wherein dwelt Black Roderick, she saw the great changes that had come to pass therein, for the day that had fallen to her in paradise was as seven years on earth.

With her death had come strife and disunion among the clans, and now at the walls stood the soldiers of her father, and within on his death-bed the Black Earl who was dying, a prisoner in their hands.

And as the little bride came to the gates of the garden without the courtyard, she saw before them a strange and horrible coach. And the only light that came from this dark carriage was from the red eyes of the six horses who drew it, and their trappings swept the ground, black and mouldy. Now, the body of this coach was shaped like a coffin, and at the head sat the driver.

When the little bride gazed upon him in wonder who he could be, she saw through the misty winding-sheet that enfolded him a death's head. But when she looked at him who sat at the foot of the coffin, she hid her face, for it was an evil creature who crouched here.

Now, as the little bride paused at the gate of the garden a voice came from inside, and said:

"Wherefore comest thou?"

And he who sat at the foot of the coffin answered:

"Open, for I claim the soul of Black Roderick."

And the voice that was within answered:

"Thou shalt come, for his cruelty hath driven my young daughter to her grave, wherein she lieth while the birds sing, and the flowers blossom, and the earth is glad with youth and spring."

So he dropped the bolt and the door swung open, so the coach and its six horses entered.

Now, when the driver reached the door of the court-yard, he found it closed against him, and he drew his coach up beside it and called in a hollow voice for entrance.

And one cried from inside:

"Wherefore comest thou?"

And he who was inside answered:

"I claim the soul of Black Roderick."

And the voice replied:

"Willingly do I open, for he hath slain my sweet sister with his chill heart and cruel ways, so she lieth in the dark earth who was the sunshine of our house."

Then the door swung open so the black coach and its six horses could enter.

Again the strange coach drove on, till it came to the castle door, and there the evil being who was inside cast himself upon the ground, and, going to the door, knocked thereon three times, and a woman's voice answered, saying:

"Who art thou?"

And the evil one replied:

"I am he who claims the soul of Black Roderick."

And the woman said:

"Welcome thou art, then, for he hath destroyed my heart's treasure and buried it in the ground; so I go sorrowing all my days for the suffering he caused her on earth, and for her young and unready death."

Then the bolts and the bars fell from the door with a great noise, and the evil thing entered the castle.

Now, as Black Roderick lay upon his death-bed tossing and turning in his fever, there rushed unto him one of the serving-men in a great terror and fear.

And of what they spoke together shall I sing thee, lest thou grow weary of my prose:

There is one at the door, O my master,
At the door, who is bidding you come!
Who is he that wakes me in the darkness,
Calling when all the world's dumb?

Six horses has he to his carriage,
Six horses blacker than the night;

And their twelve red eyes in the shadows
Twelve lamps he carries for his light.

And his coach is a coffin black and mouldy,
A huge oak coffin open wide;
He asks for your soul, God have mercy!
Who is calling at the door outside.

Who let him through the gates of my garden,
Where stronger bolts have never been?
'Twas the father of the fair little lady
You drove to her grave so green.

And who let him pass through the court-yard,
By loosening the bar and chain?
Oh, who but the brother of your mistress
Who lies in the cold and the rain!

Then who drew the bolts at the portal
And into my house bade him go?
She, the mother of the poor little colleen
Who lies in her youth so low.

Who stands that he dare not enter
The door of my chamber between?
Oh, the ghost of the fair little lady
Who lies in the church-yard green.

Now, when the evil one saw the spirit of the young bride at the door, her arms spread out in the form of a cross, he did not know what to do. And had not Black Roderick, in his joy and desire, sprung from his bed on hearing the voice of his mistress bidding him fear not, all perchance had gone well.

But Roderick, sick and eager for the sight of his bride, flung open the door, and was seized by the evil one and carried away. Now, the spirit of the little bride followed the horrible coach that contained her love, even to the flaming gates of hell, and there the evil one stopped and looked upon her with desire.

"Better," quoth he, "a thousand times to let go this wretched fellow, who will surely return to me later, if I can gain this soul who hath come even out of the kingdom of heaven."

And, turning to the poor little bride, he said: "Give thou thyself to me, and I will let this love of thine return to the world to work out his redemption."

But the little soul, weeping, saith:

"Nay, my soul belongeth to Christ in heaven, and I must not give it to thee; but for seven years shall I be thy slave if thou givest this dear one to me at the end."

So the evil one thought to himself: "Would I could steal this white soul from heaven to be the greatest gem in my crown of triumph, and to serve me seven years. At the end of that time her heart will incline to evil, and she will become mine."

And again she spoke to him, and of what she said I shall sing thee, lest thou grow weary of my prose:

If you will let his young soul go free,
I will serve you true and well,
For seven long years to be your slave
In the bitterest place of hell.

"Seven long years if you be my slave
I will let his soul go free."
The stranger drew her then by the hand,
And into the night went he.

Seven long years did she serve him true
By the blazing gates of hell,
And on every soul that entered in
The tears of her sorrow fell.

Seven long years did she keep the place
To open the doors accurst,
And every soul that her tear-drops knew,
It would neither burn nor thirst.

And once she let in her father dear,
And once her brother through.
Once came a friend she had loved full well:
Oh, bitter it was to do!

Now, no toil in the great halls of the evil one could have been more bitter to endure than to unbar the door for the lost souls; for her sweet tenderness was tortured most of all by the despairing ghosts that passed to their eternal perdition, and her hands felt guilty at letting them go through.

But of all the sorrows none was so great as for her eyes to see the tortures of Black Roderick, who stood beside her in his anguish, for the tears that fell upon him from her eyes gave him no relief, since he had injured her on earth. She held her hands to hold the fiery waters that fell upon him, and her tender body strove to stand between him and his tortures in vain. Seeing her so endeavoring, the evil one spoke, saying:

"What hast thou about thee, little soul, that thou art free from my fire and torments?"

Then the little bride remembered the tears she had hidden in her heart, that had fallen upon her in heaven from the angel's eyes, and she drew them forth.

And the tears spoke to her, saying:

"Put us not away, lest the torments overpower thee, so thou mayst never come to the kingdom of heaven."

But the little bride lifted them upon the heart and mouth of Black Roderick, so he suffered no more the cruel tortures of the lost. Now, when the evil one saw this, he smiled to himself, "For," quoth he, "now will she know temptations, since she hath put away the angel's tears, and hath no protection save her own strength."

And so bitter were her sufferings that the little bride cried out it was more than she could bear.

And the evil one, hearing her, said:

"Give thyself to me, and thou shalt suffer no more."

But she turned her face away, and made him no answer.

Then Black Roderick, looking upon her, saw her anguish, and to his soul came such bitter repentance that great tears fell from his eyes upon her, and every tear was as balm upon her sad and suffering flesh. So that when the seven years were over she stood whole and without pain.

Now, when the seven long years were at an end, she found the naming doors opened of themselves for her and Black Roderick to go forth. But when she took her love by the hand, a great cry rose from the lost souls she had let into the burning place during her seven years of trial. And in her heart was such grief she could not go. She heard her father's voice call to her, and the voice of her brother. Therefore went she to the throne of the evil one, and begged him to grant her a boon.

"For I have worked long for thee and well," quoth she, "and I beg of thee to let me carry forth as much treasure as my strength can bear."

"That," saith he, "thou shalt have; all thou canst carry thou mayst take forth, if thou wilt give me for payment seven more years of service."

Now, when the little bride heard this she bowed her head and wept.

"Seven long years," saith she, "shall I serve thee more." She took Black Roderick by the hand, and stood by him at the open doors. "Go thou upward," saith she, "and await me in heaven."

Then she closed the flaming gates, and took her place behind them. But the soul of Black Roderick crouched outside, as a dog lieth on the threshold of his master. For seven long years he let no one approach the naming gates, so that not once were they opened during the last seven years of her trial. And when the day came for her to go forth, the little bride flung the gates apart with a loud cry of joy. She knew the evil one could but grant the promise she had extorted, for she had served him well.

And of the further trials and temptations that came to her shall I sing thee, lest thou grow weary of my prose:

Seven long years did she serve him well
Until the last day was done;

And all the souls she had let in.
They clung to her one by one.

And all the souls she had let through,
They clung to her dress and hair,
Until the burden that she brought forth
Was heavy as she could bear.

The first who stopped upon her way
Was a Saint all fair to see,
And "Sister, your load is great," she said,
"So give it, I pray, to me."

"Brigit I am; God sent me forth
That you to your love might go"--
The woman she drew the fair robe aside,
And a cloven hoof did show.

"And I will not give it to you," she said,
Quick grasping her burden tight;
And all the souls that surrounded her
Clung closer in dire affright.

The next who stopped her upon her way
Was an angel with sword aflame;
"The Lord has sent for your load," he said:
"St. Michael it is my name."

The woman drew back his gown of white,
And the cloven hoof did see.
"Oh, God be with me this day," she said,
"For bitter my sorrows be."

"And I will not give it to you," she said,
And wept full many a tear.
And all the souls that her burden made
Cried out in desperate fear.

Now, the spirit of the poor little bride stopped upon her way, and feared to go farther, for she knew not what to do nor where to go, and it seemed as though there were none to trust. And as she stood, with the trembling souls clinging to her, from the far-off earth came the sweet singing of a robin; and as the bird sang he came nearer and nearer, till the little bride could see his red throat pulsing with his song. And the song he bore upon his beak was her mother's prayer.

Now, when the soul of the little bride heard this sweet singing, she became strong, and followed the bird even to the gates of heaven; and there she paused, trembling, afraid to knock, for she had gone forth of her own free will, and she had returned with a burden that she had no leave to bring.

"And without these dear ones how could I enter?" saith she; and the souls trembled with her in her fear.

But the robin tapped upon the golden gates three times with his beak, and flung his song into the shining blue of the skies.

Then a voice came forth, saying:

"By what right comest thou, of all birds, to disturb the peace of paradise with thy singing?"

And the robin answered:

"Because I alone, of all birds, strove to draw forth the cruel nails in Calvary; so my breast is ever red with the sacred blood."

"And what song bearest thou upon thy bill," saith the voice, "that would be welcome here?"

"The prayer of a mother for the soul of her little child," quoth the robin.

When he saith this the doors of paradise were opened, and upon the threshold stood one of the archangels of the Lord, and his face was glad and glorious as the sun. And when he saw the little bride, with her burden of trembling souls clinging to her dress and hair, he bade her enter.

"Thou hast done well," saith he, "and there is joy in heaven over thy return."

And as he led her by the hand the souls dropped from her and flew through the golden gates with loud cries of joy.

So brought she to heaven the soul of Black Roderick, that had been lost but for her great and suffering love. And from the closed gates none came forth save the little robin.

Now must I end my tale, lest thou grow weary of the telling.

And if more thou requirest, listen thou to the robin, who alone of all birds hath seen the glories of paradise, and who telleth to all men, if they would but hear, his pride and his joy. Even in winter, when snow and hunger chill him almost to death, when all other birds are silent with discontent, he sitteth upon a low bough and telleth the story of Black Roderick and his little bride, and of many things good to the heart of man. Listen thou and hearken.

Dora Sigerson Shorter – A Concise Bibliography

Poetry Collections
Verses (1893)
The Fairy Changeling and Other Poems (1897)
The Collected Poems of Dora Sigerson Shorter (1907)
New Poems (1913)
The Sad Years (1918)

The Tricolour, Poems of the Irish Revolution (1922)

Novels
The Country-House Party (1905)
The Story and Song of Black Roderick (1906)
Through Wintry Terrors (1907)

Short Story collections
The Father Confessor, Stories of Death and Danger (1900)